A Note to Parents

For many children, learning m[...] math!" is their first response — to [...] add "Me, too!" Children often see adults comfortably reading and writing, but they rarely have such models for mathematics. And math fear can be catching!

The easy-to-read stories in this **Hello Math Reader!** series were written to give children a positive introduction to mathematics and parents a pleasurable re-acquaintance with a subject that is important to everyone's life. **Hello Math Reader!** stories make mathematical ideas accessible, interesting, and fun for children. The activities and suggestions at the end of each book provide parents with a hands-on approach to help children develop mathematical interest and confidence.

Enjoy the mathematics!

• Give your child a chance to retell the story. The more familiar children are with the story, the more they will understand its mathematical concepts.
• Use the colorful illustrations to help children "hear and see" the math at work in the story.
• Treat the math activities as games to be played for fun. Follow your child's lead. Spend time on those activities that engage your child's interest and curiosity.
• Activities, especially ones using physical materials, help make abstract mathematical ideas concrete.

Learning is a messy process and learning about math calls for children to become immersed in lively experiences that help them make sense of mathematical concepts and symbols.

Although learning about numbers is basic to math, other ideas, such as identifying shapes and patterns, measuring, collecting and interpreting data, reasoning logically, and thinking about chance are also important. By reading these stories and having fun with the activities, you will help your child enthusiastically say **"Hello, math,"** instead of "I hate math."

—Marilyn Burns
National Mathematics Educator
Author of *The I Hate Mathematics! Book*

For Gram, our best lemonade customer
— C.W.

For Zart and Christel, Giovanni and Alessandra
— C.O.

ISBN 0-439-30475-X

Copyright © 2002 by Scholastic Inc.
The activities on pages 27-32 copyright © 2002 by Marilyn Burns.
All rights reserved. Published by Scholastic Inc.
SCHOLASTIC, HELLO MATH READER, CARTWHEEL BOOKS, and associated logos are trademarks and/or registered trademarks of Scholastic Inc.

Library of Congress Cataloging-in-Publication Data

Weiskopf, Catherine.
    Lemon & ice & everything nice! / by Catherine Weiskopf ; illustrated by Cristina Ong ; math activities by Marilyn Burns.
        p.   cm. — (Hello math reader!. Level 3)
    "Cartwheel books."
    Summary: Two best friends open a lemonade stand to earn money for matching pairs of pink sunglasses, but they have a hard time determining what a glass of lemonade is worth. Includes math problems and a lemonade recipe.
    ISBN 0-439-30475-X
    [1. Moneymaking projects — Fiction. 2. Money — Fiction. 3. Best friends — Fiction. 4. Lemonade — Fiction.] I. Title: Lemon & ice & everything nice!.
    II. Ong, Cristina, ill. III. Burns, Marilyn. IV. Title. V. Series.
    PZ7.W44637 Le 2002
    [Fic] — dc21   2001020816

10 9 8 7 6 5 4 3 2 1   02 03 04 05 06

Printed in the U.S.A.   24
First printing, April 2002

Lemon & Ice & Everything Nice

by Catherine Weiskopf
Illustrated by Cristina Ong
Math Activities by Marilyn Burns

Hello Math Reader! — Level 3

Cartwheel
·B·O·O·K·S· ®

SCHOLASTIC INC.
New York   Toronto   London   Auckland   Sydney   Mexico City
New Delhi   Hong Kong   Buenos Aires

Ming put a pitcher and paper cups on a small table. Her best friend Chelle wrote the word lemonade on a sign. "Okay!" she said. "We're open for business."

"Wait," said Ming. "How much should we charge for our lemonade?"

"We only need to make $5.00," Chelle answered. "Then those two pairs of pink sunglasses from the neighbor's garage sale are ours!"

"I saw a bottle of water for $1.50 at the zoo yesterday," Ming said.

"I'm sure lemonade costs more than water," said Chelle. She wrote "$3.00 a glass" on the sign.

"If we make the lemonade really, really cold, we can charge more," Ming said.

lemonade
~~$3.00~~ a glass
~~$4.00~~
$5.00

"We'll need ice," said Chelle. She crossed out "$3.00" and wrote "$4.00" on the sign.

"If we serve it with a straw and a slice of lemon, I'll bet we can charge even more," Ming said. She ran inside and came back with ice, straws, and lemons. Chelle fixed the sign one more time. Then both girls shouted:

"Ice-cold lemonade! $5.00 a glass!"

Ming waited by the money box. "All we need is one customer," she said.

"Hey, you look like you need a glass of lemonade," Chelle called to a girl pushing a lawn mower down the street.

"I sure am thirsty," the girl said. "And I just got paid $10.00 for mowing. But I'm saving this money for a movie. If I spend half of it on lemonade, I can't get popcorn and a drink." The girl kept walking.

"Ice-cold lemonade — $5.00 a glass!"
Chelle shouted.

"Ice-cold, as expensive as gold,"
someone shouted back.

"Oh, no!" Chelle groaned.

lemonade
$3.00 a glass
$4.00
$5.00

Chelle's brother Kyle came rolling by on his bicycle. He parked right in front of the girls' table. He looked at Chelle's sign.

"Five dollars a glass!" Kyle said. "I could buy 10 candy bars or 5 bottles of juice for that. Lemonade, ice-cold, as expensive as . . ."

"Ming, did you hear someone compare our wonderful lemonade to gold?" asked Chelle. The girls gave each other high fives. Kyle rode away.

Ming and Chelle waited and waited.

"All we need is one customer," Chelle said.

"All we have is zero customers," Ming said.

"The salesperson, that's me," said Chelle, "requests a meeting with the treasurer, that's you."

"We'll start with a treasurer's report," Ming said. "We haven't made any money."

"I know," said Chelle, "that's why I called this meeting. I think we need to have a sale. We could sell 5 glasses of lemonade for $1.00 each."

"We could call it a one-hour sale," said Ming.

"One-hour sale on ice-cold lemonade," the girls shouted.

"One glass, $1.00," Chelle called to a passing neighbor.

"Sorry, Chelle, but this dollar is for a loaf of bread," the neighbor replied.

"Uh-oh, Chelle! Look over there," Ming said. Kyle skateboarded past the lemonade stand.

"One-hour sale on ice-cold empty your billfold lemonade?" he cried. "No way! I'd rather have 2 candy bars than 1 of your lemonades."

"Ming, did you hear someone say he'd empty his billfold for a glass of our lemonade, it's so good?" Chelle asked.

The girls laughed. Kyle rolled away.

lemonade
~~$3.00~~ a glass
~~$4.00~~
~~$5.00~~
$1.00

An hour passed.

"Our lemonade is going to get warm," said Chelle.

"The treasurer," Ming said, "requests a meeting with the salesperson. The money box is still empty. How can I continue to be the treasurer without any money to treasure?"

"Any ideas?" Chelle asked.

"Another sale," said Ming. "A moving sale!"

"But we aren't moving," said Chelle.

"We could move the business across the street later," answered Ming. "Let's charge 50¢ a glass now."

"Two pairs of perfect pink sunglasses cost $5.00," Chelle reminded her friend.

"So we have to sell 10 glasses of lemonade at our new price," Ming said.

"Moving sale!" Chelle yelled.

A woman and her son were working in their front yard across the street. They heard Chelle. They put down their rakes and walked towards the two girls. The woman read the sign.

"Fifty cents a glass," she read. "We'll take 2 lemonades, please." The woman handed Ming 4 quarters. "I didn't know both of your families were moving. We'll miss you in the neighborhood."

"Actually, we're just thinking of moving our business to the corner," Ming replied.

"Pssst," said Chelle. She pointed down the street. "Look who's coming."

Kyle raced by on a scooter. "Ice-cold, very old lemonade," he sang out. "I'd still rather have 1 sweet, creamy candy bar than 1 sour, old lemonade."

"Ming, did you hear someone say he wasn't old enough to drink lemonade as fine as ours?" Chelle asked.

The two girls bent over laughing. Kyle frowned and lost his balance. The scooter wobbled.

Another hour passed. Chelle and Ming were hot. Ming had gone inside for more ice cubes, twice. But the girls had still only sold 2 lemonades.

"I call another meeting," Chelle said. "Let's go right to the treasurer's report."

"So far we have made $1.00," Ming said.

"We need to make $4.00 more," said Chelle.

lemonade
a glass

$3.00
$4.00
$5.00
$1.00
50¢
25¢

"I think we should have another sale, the biggest sale ever, a clearance sale!" Ming said.

"How much should we charge?" asked Chelle.

"We want everybody to buy our lemonade," replied Ming. "How about 25¢ a glass?"

"That means we have to sell 4 lemonades to earn a dollar, and we need to earn $4.00," replied Ming.

"That means selling 16 lemonades," Chelle said.

The two girls looked at each other.

"Clearance sale!" shouted Ming.

"Get your ice-cold lemonade!" shouted Chelle. "Twenty-five cents a glass!"

HONK!!!

Kyle pulled up in his toy car. "Twenty-five cents and ice-cold? I'm sold!" he said. He handed a quarter to Ming.

"Sold for 25¢ to the boy who's hot and thirsty from bothering us." Chelle grinned.

Ming handed Kyle a glass of lemonade. He gulped it down.

"This ice-cold lemonade is worth 25¢ a glass!" Kyle said. A real car stopped behind him.

"Lemonade? We'll take 4," the driver said. He handed Ming 4 quarters. Chelle and Ming were very busy for the next half hour.

"It's time for another meeting," Ming said.
"We need to count our money."

"And we're almost out of lemonade,"
added Chelle.

The two girls counted their money. They
had 2 one-dollar bills, 12 quarters, 5 dimes,
and 10 nickels.

"We made $6.00," Ming said. "That means we have one extra dollar!"

"Let's go buy those sunglasses!" said Chelle.

Ming and Chelle crossed the street to
the garage sale. "We're here to buy the matching
set of pink sunglasses," the girls said to their
neighbor.

"I'm sorry, girls," their neighbor said.
"I sold those pink sunglasses."

"But did you see these?" She waved two pairs of glittery, gold sunglasses. The frames were shaped like flowers.

"These sunglasses are even cooler than the pink ones," said Chelle.

"How much are they?" asked Ming.

"I'll give you both pairs for $6.50," the neighbor answered.

"Oh no, we only have $6.00," Ming said.

"Wait, I've got an idea," said Chelle. "I'll be right back." She raced across the street . . .

and came back with 2 glasses of lemonade.

"How about $6.00 and 2 glasses of ice-cold lemonade?" Chelle asked.

"Ice-cold, as good as gold . . . sunglasses!" said Ming.

"Sold!" said the neighbor.

• ABOUT THE ACTIVITIES •

Although children become aware of money at an early age, it's harder for them to understand how our monetary system works. There are several reasons for this. The names of coins—penny, nickel, dime, or quarter—don't give children clues about their value. Having more coins doesn't necessarily mean having more money. While a dime is a small coin, it's worth more than a nickel or a penny, two larger-sized coins. Despite these difficulties, learning about money is important for children. Not only is understanding our monetary system a basic, real-world skill, experience with money helps develop children's number sense and computational ability, especially with mental arithmetic. Figuring out how many 25-cent glasses of lemonade the girls need to sell to earn $5.00, for example, builds children's skill with numerical reasoning. So does counting up a collection of change to figure out how much money is there.

Children benefit from having many opportunities to use money for solving problems in real-world and play situations. The activities in this section suggest some ways for you to provide that experience for your child. First, gather a collection of coins to have on hand: 2 silver or gold dollars, 6 quarters, 10 dimes, 20 nickels, and at least 50 pennies. Then enjoy the activities with your child!

—Marilyn Burns

You'll find tips and suggestions for guiding the activities whenever you see a box like this!

Retelling the Story

Ming and Chelle wanted to earn $5.00 to buy pink sunglasses. First they charged $3.00 for a glass of lemonade. How many glasses would they have had to sell at $3.00 to earn $5.00?

Then they charged $4.00 for a glass of lemonade. How many glasses would they have had to sell at $4.00 to earn $5.00?

Why did they finally decide to charge $5.00 for a glass of lemonade? What do you think about this price?

The girl with the lawn mower had $10.00, and she was thirsty. How much would she have had left if she'd spent $5.00 on lemonade? Why didn't she buy a glass?

Chelle's brother Kyle rolled by on his bicycle. Why didn't he buy any lemonade?

Kyle said that he could buy 10 candy bars with $5.00. How much did he think each candy bar would cost?

Kyle said that he could buy 5 bottles of juice with $5.00. How much did he think each bottle of juice would cost?

What happens when Ming and Chelle decide to have a one-hour sale and sell lemonade for $1.00 a glass?

Chelle's brother Kyle skateboarded past the lemonade stand. Why didn't he buy some lemonade?

Ming and Chelle then decided to have a moving sale. They charged 50¢ a glass. They planned to move their business across the street later. Ming thought that they would have to sell 10 glasses of lemonade to earn $5.00. How did she figure this?

The girls sold two 50-cent glasses of lemonade to a woman and her son. The woman handed Ming 4 quarters. How much did they earn for these 2 glasses? How much more did they need to earn to buy the sunglasses for $5.00?

Chelle's brother Kyle raced by on a scooter. Why didn't he buy some lemonade?

Ming and Chelle decided to have another sale — a clearance sale — and charge 25¢ for a glass of lemonade. What is a clearance sale?

Chelle thought that they would have to sell 16 glasses of lemonade to earn $4.00. How did she figure this out?

Chelle's brother Kyle pulled up in his toy car. What did he do?

Then a real car pulled up. The driver handed Ming 4 quarters for four 25-cent glasses of lemonade. How much did the girls earn for these four glasses?

After half an hour, the girls had 2 one-dollar bills, 12 quarters, 5 dimes, and 10 nickels. They figured that they had $6.00. How did they count their money?

What happened when the girls went to buy the pink sunglasses?

The Four Quarters Problem

The woman and her son paid 4 quarters for 2 glasses of lemonade that cost 50¢ each. The driver of the car paid 4 quarters for 4 glasses of lemonade that cost 25¢ each.

How many glasses of lemonade could you buy with 4 quarters if lemonade cost 20¢ a glass? What if lemonade cost 10¢ a glass? 5¢ a glass? 2¢? 1¢? Make a chart like the one below.

Lemonade for 4 Quarters

Cost for a Glass	Glasses of Lemonade
50¢	2
25¢	4
20¢	?
10¢	?
5¢	?
1¢	?

Using real money can help your child figure out these problems and verify that their answers are correct. Experience with real money will help your child learn how to compute with coins abstractly.

Another Four Quarters Problem

Four quarters is equal to $1.00. You can make $1.00 with other coins: 100 pennies, 20 nickels, 10 dimes, or a 1 dollar coin. And you can make $1.00 by mixing different coins. For example, 2 quarters and 5 dimes make $1.00. So do 3 quarters, 2 dimes, and 1 nickel. Try to find other combinations of coins that equal $1.00.

Be sure to provide your child with a collection of coins for this problem. It may be helpful if you model for your child how you count a collection of coins, starting with the larger denominations first and then adding the coins of lower values.

Making Lemonade

Here's a recipe for making one glass of lemonade.

2 tablespoons fresh lemon juice
1 1/2 tablespoons sugar
1 cup water
Put in a glass and stir to dissolve sugar. Add ice to chill.

     Suppose you opened a lemonade stand and wanted to make enough lemonade for 10 glasses. How much lemon juice would you need?
How much sugar?
How much water?
     If you sold 10 glasses of lemonade at 25¢ a glass, how much money would you earn? What if you charged 50¢ a glass?
     Figure out how much you would earn if you charged other amounts.

If you have a computer, you can find several lemonade stand games where your child can play at figuring out the costs and profits of running a lemonade stand. Type "Lemonade Stand Game" into any online search engine for a list of web sites.